MW00957899

The Gentleman's Impertinent Daughter

A Pride and Prejudice Novella Variation

By Rose Fairbanks

The Gentleman's Impertinent Daughter

Rose Fairbanks

Published by Rose Fairbanks

Early drafts were written in 2013 and posted serially beginning October 20, 2013 and ending November 29, 2013.

Several passages in this novel are paraphrased from the works of Jane Austen.

ISBN-13: 978-1500396862

ISBN-10: 1500396869

Chapter 1

"Come Brother, let us rest ourselves for a moment," Georgiana Darcy beseeched her elder brother. The two settled on a nearby bench.

"I am sorry Sweetling. It is very warm and I should be more attentive to you. Would you like to go home?" Fitzwilliam Darcy looked at his sister with concern. The sun was shining unseasonably hot for late September.

"No, I am well."

"I do wish you would come with me to Hertfordshire, or allow me to stay behind with you. I do not like leaving you after your ordeal just yet."

They had arrived in London only two days before, after celebrating the customary Michaelmas feast at Pemberley, their country estate. After the betrayal of the summer and the hustle of the harvest, Darcy

3

was looking forward to enjoying a holiday, but hated to leave his dear sister behind.

"Really, William, it was not an illness. I have simply had low spirits because of my foolishness."

Georgiana lowered her voice. "I would enjoy the countryside but I will take the cowardly way out and avoid Mr. Bingley's sisters since you offered. You know how difficult it is for me to make new friends and I do not trust my judgment in regards to their sincerity anymore. Therefore I would be trapped with the ladies all day and make you feel guilty for any enjoyment you experience. No, you go. You work so hard. Mrs. Annesley and I shall see you at Christmas."

After a short pause she added, "Now, I think I shall watch the ducks just down there."

Mr. Darcy watched his baby sister leave. She had grown into a beautiful young lady while he was unawares. Early in the summer she had been taken advantage of, her heart broken asunder, by his childhood best friend and very own father's godson.

Swept away by romance she believed herself in love and consented to an elopement.

Learning the man in question only desired her stout dowry of thirty thousand pounds and revenge on her brother made her feelings of guilt even worse than when she understood the gravity of the scandal her actions would have caused. She had not recovered her spirits and was still filled with shame and melancholy.

I was charged to protect her and I have failed her.

Nearby he heard something wholly unexpected, a full, hearty laugh from a woman. It had been years since he heard a woman laugh so openly, not since his mother's death. And the tone of this particular laugh was delightful and enchanting. Women of his circle rarely laughed unless they were belittling someone. It was a sad way to live, to be so bitter and angry.

His eyes sought out the owner of the musical laughter and saw a young woman surrounded by four children under the age of ten.

Surely she is much too young to be their mother but dressed too fine to be a governess. Though clearly she takes little care of her wardrobe, given the way she romps with the little mites. Refreshing, a young lady not interested in fashion.

He had never seen a woman with such obvious zest for life before. This lady had an inner happiness and was unafraid for the world to see it.

"Again, Cousin Lizzy! Again!" the smallest lad cried demandingly as she took him in her arms and spun around. Setting him down in laughter, two older women approached her.

One stayed with the children and the other walked with the young lady towards a bench near his. Darcy was shocked by the tugging in his heart. He felt regret in the assuredness of never witnessing a similar scene at his own home. *Will my own children be happier than I was?*

He had no intention of eavesdropping but a very familiar name caught his attention. "All Mr. Collins could speak of was his patroness, Lady Catherine de

Bourgh," said the younger lady, 'Cousin Lizzy.'

She continued, "Thankfully Mama directed him away from Jane to start with, as Mama believes Jane must be saved for an illustrious match given her beauty. Not that I feared she would accept him anyway. You know Jane and I have vowed to never marry but for love and we could barely tolerate his sycophantic ways.

"Whatever came over my friend, Charlotte, to accept him I truly will never understand. But I thank you for allowing me to visit; Mama was becoming unbearable."

"Of course, dear. We are always happy to have you. And shall you return to us in January?" the older woman asked.

Cousin Lizzy snorted. "You know very well I never want another London Season. I do not care for Town at all but for the theatres, museums and bookshops. After turning down Mr. Collins, Mama has despaired of me ever marrying and has decided to send Kitty in my place. I am not sure if Mary should feel disappointed at being overlooked or relieved!"

She laughed and then sobered a little. "Truly, I believe Mama is correct. No man shall have me for none respect me. I have practically no portion, a vulgar family, no connections and am certainly not handsome enough to tempt one otherwise."

"Now, Elizabeth, you have not met very many men and are only twenty. This smacks of bitterness."

"Oh, Aunt Gardiner, I just feel as though I do not fit in anywhere, never valued for myself. I am impertinent and wild and do not wish to change."

"Some gentlemen prefer outspoken ladies with frankness and you are never improper or mean; indeed there is a playful sweetness about you. And wild? I have never seen evidence of that."

"Well, I did walk three miles to Netherfield in the mud to check on Jane last month." Glancing down at herself she told her aunt, "I arrived looking very much like this now and I know Miss Bingley and Mrs. Hurst held me in contempt for it. But Jane was ill and needed me and the carriage was not to be had. I have yet to have the patience to truly master riding and so I walked."

Darcy had been fascinated by the conversation before but he recognized the name of the estate she mentioned as the very one leased by his best friend. The very place he intended to travel to on the morrow. Hearing her care for her sister resonated with his heart.

If I ever marry, I would want her to be a true sister to Georgie, with affection like this young miss has for her sister.

He then stole a look at her, given the fact that she knew his best friend and believed his sister hated her. He had no difficulty believing that. Caroline Bingley hated most people.

Elizabeth's face was bright and animated by the exercise and conversation. Her eyes were vibrant and danced in the sunlight.

Her aunt replied, "I would never call those actions wild, though perhaps unwise. As for Mr. Bingley's sisters I am sure you can handle them with all the grace and poise you exhibit in the hostile environment of London drawing rooms. Some of the ladies I must visit are terribly dreadful and you are never improper.

"Additionally, you explained Mr. Bingley took the sudden lease at Netherfield instead of going to a fashionable resort for the month of August. His sisters were likely to be displeased by everything out of sheer disappointment."

Patting her niece on the hand she continued, "Now, let us speak of better things. Will you come with us on the lake journey next summer?"

"Yes, you know not how I anticipate it."

"Very good. Among other stops we plan on visiting my childhood home in Lambton."

Darcy could scarce believe his ears. This young lady knew his best friend, his aunt's parson, and her aunt grew up a mere five miles from his estate and would be visiting the area the following summer.

"You will want to see Pemberley, I am sure. I believe Derbyshire to be the finest of all the counties and Pemberley's house is my favourite. But the grounds! Lizzy, we will have to drag you away."

Elizabeth laughed at this, "I do look forward to it then! Tell me more about Derbyshire. Does uncle still plan to buy an estate there soon?"

Darcy frowned; although both ladies were dressed finely she apparently was in trade. It mattered not; surely he had no intentions towards a stranger. *Though when I arrive at Netherfield she will no longer be one...*

"Yes, we could have earlier but the continued war with Napoleon makes him want to wait so he can better manage his affairs from afar."

"I think it so brave of you and uncle to have taken the Import/Export opportunity."

"You know your uncle. Grandson to a gentleman but his father disliked Town and chose to become a country lawyer as the usual lot of second sons did not appeal to him. Your uncle came so late to your grandfather's life the law practice was already promised to Mr. Phillips after your other uncle's unexpected death."

She paused for a moment and added, "I think we both know that he is far happier in his current profession than he would be as an attorney."

So, a second son of a second son, that is...respectable.

"And what of you? Surely the Greenes expected you to marry a gentleman."

"And so your uncle is! I do not hold with the belief that because he manages a business instead of land he has lost his rank due his birth."

"Besides, we make too much of birth. No one is born with superior behaviour, they are taught it through education and many tradesmen these days can better afford expensive schooling than peers." Elizabeth stated emphatically.

Darcy reeled at the words: astonishing, unpopular and thought provoking. She did not sound like a revolutionary, simply a pragmatist. Is not my friend Bingley proof of this? Not to mention my aunt, born daughter of an earl, can be quite vulgar.

Elizabeth began again with gusto, "The world is changing. The tradesmen are propelling technology and industry which is creating capital needed to fund the incessant wars and colonisation, which is not as entirely profitable as the lords would have us think. Meanwhile people are leaving the estates and making goods in their homes to try their luck at wealth in the cities.

"Fortunately few of our tenants have left, but I worry for those that do. The cities are cruel and there is no one to aid them. Our estate is not vast or very profitable, although I attribute at least some of that to my father's indolence as he hates the entailment. At any rate, what we do have we owe to our tenants and in turn we treat them very well."

Darcy breathed out a sigh of relief. She was a gentleman's daughter after all. Clearly not one of any importance, as he knew of no one noteworthy that resided near his friend's estate, but they were...equals. Yes, equals. My relations might be nobles but I am not.

"Very wise, as always, my dear. But come, let us gather the children."

Darcy was struck with their conversation and was dwelling on the prospect of a pair of very fine eyes in the face of a pretty and very astute, intelligent woman. All worries for his sister slipped away, for the first time in months.

*****

Georgiana Darcy left her brother on the park bench and made her way to the pond. Watching the ducks she said a silent prayer. She desired a friend, a true confidante and perhaps a sister. *A good wife for William and a sister for me.*

She spied four children and their governess frolicking and tossing a ball when it went astray, near her. She bent to retrieve it and walked towards the group of children.

"Here you are dear," she spoke to the youngest boy.

"Thank you. Are you an angel?" the little one asked.

"Master Michael!" The governess chided.

Laughing, Georgiana intervened, "No, he is charming. No, little one, I am not an angel. What makes you think so?"

"Your hair is made of gold! Even prettier than Cousin Jane! What is your name, Angel?"

"Master Michael, such poor manners!" the governess reprimanded again.

"But my name is an angel and so is Gabe's and the girls are named after Grandmama and Grandmother and Mama says they are angels watching us from Heaven and all of our cousins are named for other angels in Heaven..."

Georgiana laughed again, "Actually, Master Michael I am named for my mother and father, George and Anne Darcy, and they are both now angels in Heaven too."

Mrs. Gardiner and Elizabeth approached with every intention of chiding Michael as well and overheard Georgiana's last statement. Mrs. Gardiner could not contain her delight upon hearing who conversed with her children.

"Excuse me, did I hear correctly? Are you Miss Georgiana Darcy of Pemberley?" At Mrs. Gardiner's approach the governess walked towards the other children.

15

Startled and shy speaking with the ladies instead of the child, she looked at her feet and spoke softly. "Yes, I am."

From his bench Darcy happened to view the scene and began to move in their direction.

Mrs. Gardiner tried to ease Georgiana's embarrassment. "Forgive me, I do not mean to make you uneasy. You see I grew up near Lambton and remember meeting your family a few times."

Georgiana's head jerked up in delighted surprise, "Really? You met my father and mother?"

"Yes, a sweeter woman who loved her family and tenants I have yet to meet. And you, dear, are just as beautiful."

Mr. Darcy reached Georgiana just then. "Georgiana, are you well?"

"Oh, yes, William! She was just telling me about Mother!" Georgiana beamed at her brother.

He attempted to conceal his excitement at a reason to speak with the pretty young lady. "How delightful. Could you introduce me to your new friends?" At this his sister reddened in embarrassment.

Mrs. Gardiner intervened again, "Forgive us sir. I happened upon Miss Darcy as she was speaking with my children and was too delighted to make an acquaintance from my childhood home to remember the essentials! I am Mrs. Edward Gardiner of Gracechurch Street. My husband owns the Import/Export shop on _____ Street. Perhaps you have heard of our tea?"

Quite surprised Darcy's eyebrows rose. "Indeed, Madam, my favourite in fact."

"I thank you sir. And this is my niece, Miss Elizabeth Bennet of Longbourn in Hertfordshire." Darcy forgot to breathe as Elizabeth bestowed a beautiful smile, blinding him almost like the sun.

Georgiana remembered her role. "And this is my brother, Mr. Fitzwilliam Darcy of Pemberley in Derbyshire." Darcy bowed and all the ladies curtsied.

Elizabeth replied, "A pleasure to meet you Mr. Darcy." He broke into a wide smile as she spoke. Elizabeth felt breathless at the sight of his dimples.

"Likewise, Miss Bennet."

Georgiana was oblivious to the tender moment. "Hertfordshire! Is your home anywhere near Netherfield Park? My brother's best friend, Mr. Bingley, just leased it."

"Why, yes, Longbourn is but three miles. What a coincidence! I lately had the pleasure of making Mr. Bingley's acquaintance; he is quite popular in Hertfordshire. I will be leaving tomorrow, in fact, to return."

"Tomorrow! What another coincidence. My brother and I," Georgiana stressed the last two words for Darcy to catch, "will be leaving tomorrow as well, to stay several weeks at Netherfield."

Georgiana spoke with sudden determination. "Mrs. Gardiner, we would be pleased for you and your husband and niece to dine with us this evening. I would dearly love to hear more of my mother."

It was not the usual order to extend a dinner invitation before developing the acquaintance through standard morning calls but the young lady was so endearing and excited. Additionally, she would not have a chance, possibly for months, to speak with Mrs. Gardiner again. Exchanging glances the older ladies agreed and a time was settled upon for their next meeting.

Chapter 2

Darcy walked in stunned amazement, his sister guiding him towards their townhouse. His head stumbled to understand all that transpired, but now was not the time for reflection. And reflect he surely would. That is, on the young lady's pert opinions and the shocking connections they shared; for surely he could reflect on these things without getting lost in reverie of the lady's beauty. But for now, the matter at hand was his sister and how these ladies made her blossom in a matter of minutes. She had, in fact, been livelier today than in recent months, perhaps years.

"….and he thought I was an angel! Me! I know I am not so beautiful but bless him for thinking so. And I certainly am not good at all."

"Sweetling, we have talked about this. You were deceived not only by Wickham but by your companion, Mrs. Younge. I also bear a great bit of fault as well. I should have known more of Mrs. Younge and I should have foreseen Wickham's desire for revenge. I should have explained his character to you.

"You are now a young lady, although I tend to think of you as my baby sister still. It was natural to feel attraction for Wickham, to enjoy his attentions and flattery. One must learn how to decipher a trustworthy character and in your case your protectors failed."

"But I should have known to tell you earlier. I should have known how improper a secret courtship and elopement was. I should have realized how imprudent a match it was at any rate; he has no real income."

"And how do you realize these things now, Sweetling? Because it has been explained to you. You would not know intuitively what was never said."

"But as a Darcy…"

"Stop. We have a beautiful legacy and heritage but our forefathers were just as human and flawed as we. And we certainly are not superior to others through a happy accident of birth. We simply are blessed with more worldly goods and an opportunity to better ourselves morally through education. Human nature is the same regardless of class."

"Brother, I have never heard you speak so! I have not heard you profess the opposite, but Aunt Catherine has certainly said such and at school we were taught our better birth made us innately superior."

Georgiana paused for a moment remembering the mean and condescending treatment she received at the hands of many of her own social superiors. She often felt isolated at her school and had no genuine friends, emotions which Mrs. Younge and Wickham easily exploited.

Georgiana had also often believed she would have never succumbed to Wickham's seduction if she had the superior birth of a lady; her faults indicated her lower birth. She welcomed the thought of being equal in nature to these ladies and not being intrinsically inferior was a welcome respite from her dark thoughts.

"We have discussed my transgressions many times this summer and this is the first you have mentioned this way of thinking. What has changed?"

"I think perhaps I have always known this truth, but did not know how to voice it, or if I should. I recently overheard a very intelligent young lady point out these very things and upon reflection realized she must be right. If she had the courage to speak thusly, so must I, especially since it might do my dear sister good to hear." Darcy looked tenderly upon his sister.

"Yes, I have profound relief from so astonishing a revelation. Thank you Brother." Georgiana smiled broadly.

"What did you think of Mrs. Gardiner and Miss Bennet? You know I have been worried about my sense of judgment since...since my holiday."

"You were cruelly misused by two you trusted."

"Yes, but I should have noticed the inconsistencies in their character!" Sighing, Georgiana continued. "But I do not wish to speak on that at the moment. Perhaps if I met someone else I would think my current feelings naive, but something deep within me tells me Mrs. Gardiner and Miss Bennet are genuine." And the answer to my very prayers. "I feel quite at ease with them and hope Miss Bennet and I can become great friends while I am at Netherfield."

A few more steps brought them to their London townhouse. Georgiana left to inform their housekeeper of the planned dinner guests and then her companion of the plans to accompany her brother on his travels. Mr. Darcy sent an express to Bingley informing him of two additional guests. Darcy then allowed his mind to wander over the day.

What a delightful creature she was! She seems to have done Georgiana a world of good already and they shall further their acquaintance this evening and undoubtedly in Hertfordshire. She is intelligent, beautiful and gently bred.

Darcy realized he most decidedly did not view her as only Georgiana's friend, nor could he perceive any glaring flaws in her person as he was apt to find with other young ladies. It dawned on him that he had never been so bewitched before.

*****

At the appropriate time the Gardiner party arrived. Darcy thought Elizabeth beautiful in muddied petticoats but found her captivating in evening wear.

"Miss Bennet, I must tell you how beautiful you are this evening. Is she not, Brother?"

Darcy looked towards Georgiana. It was not like her to bait him, though it was no trouble in this case to comply. He eyed his sister suspiciously and then graciously turned towards Elizabeth.

"Indeed, I must agree with my sister." Darcy said nervously. How different it feels when giving a genuine compliment!

Elizabeth blushed, only adding to her beauty. "I thank you Miss Darcy, Mr. Darcy, but I worry I do your beautiful home no justice. I did not travel with much evening wear."

"Nonsense, you honour us with your presence and your beauty is not owed to your gown. We are now friends; there is no need to feel uneasy. I prefer simple, classic cuts myself and I know my brother hates the ostentatious frippery of some of our acquaintances." Georgiana gave Elizabeth and Darcy a knowing look and all three smiled thinking of the unflattering gowns of Caroline Bingley.

"I thank you again," Elizabeth said with a smile free from her previous uncertainty.

In the time before dinner Darcy found the Gardiners very fashionable and pleasing company. During dinner Darcy wanted to hear more of Elizabeth's astute thoughts on class and tried to introduce the topic.

"It has truly been a pleasure making your acquaintance Mr. and Mrs. Gardiner. I have long enjoyed your well known tea and believe you are acquainted with some friends of mine, Mr. and Mrs. Horace Blythe, as well as Mr. Henry Scott. Along with Mr. Bingley, these are my closest friends."

"Oh, yes, very fine company indeed!" Mr. Gardiner confirmed the acquaintance. "I must say, Mr. Darcy you surprise me with the company you keep. I would have expected your acquaintances to be made up of more peers than tradesmen given your lineage."

"I find too much is made of birth. Education guides one's behaviour, not so called breeding. In my formal education I found tradesmen were not only just as capable of learning the strictures of society but they could frequently afford the cost of the institutes more easily than peers."

Darcy thought he had done quite well and expected a favourable response from Elizabeth. He was surprised to hear instead: "Ah, so you value wealth over birth then, Mr. Darcy? How very liberal of you. Perhaps one day a person may be judged on their worthiness by their wealth and thus be invited to the first circles of society by their monetary accomplishments and not merely by their birth. For why should we hope to be judged by our character?"

Have I insulted her? She has twisted my words! Darcy had placed first in debate during his time at Cambridge so instead of giving into alarm he calmly clarified. "You mistake me Miss Bennet. Many of the peers have lost their wealth and are impoverished by their own licentious practices such as gambling and that, as much as the hard work and financial diligence of many in the merchant class, proves the general character of each."

Before Elizabeth could reply Mr. Gardiner nervously intervened. "I fear you are in danger of becoming a casualty of my niece's debating skills, Mr. Darcy."

Slightly embarrassed, Elizabeth defended herself. "I was taught by my father to sometimes make arguments that are not my own and to wilfully misunderstand for the sake of debate. I pray you forgive me for my impertinence. I meant no offence."

"No forgiveness is necessary, Miss Bennet. I dare not call impertinent what is charming outspokenness of a sound mind. I am guilty of the same for a debate." He gave her an earnest look and friendly smile.

Elizabeth blushed, "You are too kind, Mr. Darcy. I know my thoughts are not always welcome and I shall take care to check my tongue."

"Pray, I always wish you to speak your mind to me and your thoughts are always welcome. There is a sweetness about you that cannot be mistaken for a caustic tongue."

Seeing her blush anew, it really is a delightful shade of pink, he redirected his thoughts. "Your father taught you debate, then? Where did he attend?"

"Cambridge, class of 1784. He placed first in debate and held the highest rank until quite recently," Elizabeth stated with pride written all over her face.

"Indeed! Your father's initials are TB, then?"

"For Thomas Bennet, yes, sir."

"How astonishing! My father was George Darcy, who placed in 1780. He briefly met your father and was very impressed. You have learned from a master indeed."

"I thank you, sir." Then Elizabeth was struck with a realization, "How did you guess my father's initials? Did you attend Cambridge as well, sir?"

"Yes, I did." Darcy began to grow uncomfortable, sensing the direction of her thoughts.

"Would you be Mr. FD who broke my father's place in 1805?"

Darcy blushed, "I am guilty of that."

"Then I greatly look forward to our travels tomorrow!" Elizabeth's eyes were twinkling in delight and she smiled with enthusiasm.

"As do I, Miss Bennet," Darcy returned the smile.

Darcy then rose and requested an adjournment to the drawing room instead of the separation of sexes. Miss Darcy invited Elizabeth and Mrs. Gardiner to perform on the pianoforte. While Mrs. Gardiner was amenable, Elizabeth attempted to decline.

"Lizzy plays and sings quite well, do not let her modesty mislead you."

"Aunt Gardiner, you really are a strange creature by way of friend! Always wanting me to play and sing before anybody and everybody! If my vanity had taken a musical turn, you would have been invaluable." On Mrs. Gardiner's persevering Elizabeth acquiesced.

Darcy found Elizabeth's performance to be quite pleasing and, though she was not an exceptional performer, her manner was easy and unaffected.

"Now, it is your turn, Miss Darcy." Elizabeth said.

"Oh, no. I am not used to performing in front of guests."

"Please, Miss Darcy? I simply must hear this beautiful instrument played as it was meant to be played."

Georgiana blushed. "Very well, but please do not ask me to sing."

"If you like." Although Elizabeth did not know Georgiana's true skill level, only having heard gossip from Mr. Bingley's sisters, she chose a piece that she knew required great expression. Soon Georgiana was lost in the music and performed exquisitely.

When she finished she looked at Elizabeth with admiration. "How did you know I would be able to perform so well despite my fears?"

"You mean besides the fact that I already know your brother would not allow any harm to ever befall you?"

Her words caused Georgiana to blush. "He is the very best brother."

Elizabeth smiled. "I knew if you could focus on the emotion of the piece you would not worry about the mechanics. You play so beautifully. I have rarely heard anything that gave me greater pleasure." She looked up from Georgiana just then and caught Darcy's eye. He was drawing near to praise his sister.

"I cannot help but agree, dear. Tonight's performances gave me more pleasure than I have heard in London's best concert halls." All the ladies blushed at the praise and Darcy hoped Elizabeth accepted his genuine compliment.

Next Mr. Darcy recommended a tour of the home which ended in the library. Elizabeth gasped in delight at the largest private collection she had ever seen.

Mrs. Gardiner laughed, "Now we shall never get her to leave!"

Darcy was surprised at how well he liked the very notion, but managed to push the thought aside. "I took you for a great reader, Miss Bennet. I am happy to see I was correct."

Elizabeth replied laughingly, "I am unsure whether you mean that as censure or praise! Yes, I do enjoy reading. I have my father's tastes."

"It could only be praise, I assure you. Please, feel free to borrow anything you find appealing. You can see they are arranged by category."

Darcy was surprised to see her browse a shelf devoted to agricultural methods. Across the room Georgiana engaged Mr. and Mrs. Gardiner on more discussions of her parents and Derbyshire. She was at perfect ease with them on the subject and Darcy was already glad to have made the acquaintance, if for no other reason than the return of his sister's cheer. Something in the back of his mind told him there was another reason to rejoice in the acquaintance and she was walking about his library in wonder.

Darcy approached Elizabeth. "And what appeals on this subject?"

"My father and I have been searching to find a particular title on the rotation method and I wondered if you might have it. The _____, have you heard of it?"

"Indeed, it is in my study now, allow me to fetch it."

"Oh, no! I would not wish to importune on something so favoured for your private use."

"Nonsense, Miss Bennet, I shall not need it in Hertfordshire and would like to be of service." Elizabeth nodded and Darcy quickly retrieved the book.

Upon returning he asked, "Are you very familiar with agricultural practices and theories?"

"Nearly as much as my father, I confess. You will not think me very accomplished, but I have an insatiable thirst for knowledge and a curiosity on nearly all topics. Much to my mother's chagrin, I cannot be occupied by the pursuit of ribbons, lace or embroidery for any length of time at all."

"I would rather Georgiana have a more substantial accomplishment than most ladies, in the improvement of her mind by extensive reading."

"And I suppose most ladies of your acquaintance can claim a thorough knowledge of music, singing, drawing, dancing and the modern languages and she possesses a certain something in her air and manner of walking, the tone of her voice, her address and expressions? Pray, how many truly accomplished young ladies do you know?"

Elizabeth recalled a list of accomplishments recited by Miss Bingley during her stay at Netherfield. Elizabeth firmly believed these ridiculous standards for measuring a woman's worth.

"I cannot boast to knowing more than half-a-dozen, in the whole range of my acquaintance, that are really accomplished." Darcy could easily see Elizabeth felt her list of accomplishments as absurd and believed she understood he referenced his own statement.

"I rather wonder at you knowing any," Elizabeth said sharply.

"Are you so severe upon your own sex as to doubt the possibility of all this?" Darcy was incredulous and stared at her in disbelief.

She confessed to being a great reader only moments ago!

Elizabeth attempted to encourage the debate. "I never saw such a woman. I never saw such capacity, and taste, and application, and elegance, as you describe united."

Realizing she was intentionally twisting his words Darcy happily clarified. "Ah, but you are the one who made the other list, mine was only of extensive reading. Allow me to add I appreciate a fine voice and skill on the pianoforte."

Dropping his voice to a whisper he boldly stated, "I assure you Miss Bennet, I indeed know at least one truly accomplished young lady, though I must admit the acquaintance is only of a matter of hours."

There! Let us see if you can wilfully misunderstand that, Miss Bennet!

Elizabeth blushed again but before she could reply was called to the carriage.

Darcy was struck with the unique shade her eyes took on during their debate. They hung between green and brown. It reminded him of a ride through the woods on a sunny day.

"Mr. Darcy, Miss Darcy, it was an honour to dine with you this evening. You must inform us of your return to Town so we might host you next."

"Mrs. Gardiner, it was very pleasant to speak with you about my parents. I fear I quite neglected Miss Bennet." Georgiana looked at Elizabeth and continued. "I truly desired to get to know you better and it would ease my mind considerably if I knew I had at least one true acquaintance in Hertfordshire when we arrive. I know this is rather forward but might you travel with us tomorrow?"

Darcy watched in amazement as Georgiana turned her eyes upon the others of the group. He recognized the expression instantly, because he could never deny her a thing when she used it. From the looks they gave each other, clearly the reaction was shared by the Gardiners and Elizabeth. His guests shared a look. It was obvious they were such a close family they needed no words.

Mrs. Gardiner answered. "It will save us having to send a maid and manservant to travel with her. What time shall you fetch Elizabeth tomorrow?"

Darcy replied looking at Elizabeth, "Would nine be too early? Georgiana prefers several hours of rest after travel before dinner."

"Oh, for Elizabeth nine is mid-morning! She is quite an early riser and enjoys taking morning walks."

"Truly, Miss Bennet? William and I rise early and enjoy a morning walk or ride as well. Perhaps in Hertfordshire you could accompany us sometime. I am certain you must know all the best paths." Georgiana showed her excitement over her new friendship with enthusiasm.

"I would be delighted, Miss Darcy. I look forward to furthering our acquaintance."

After the appropriate leave taking Mr. Gardiner was about to hand the ladies in the carriage when he realized he left his gloves in the hall. Mr. Darcy assisted the ladies instead, rather than have them wait out of doors. When his hand met Elizabeth's, he felt a shock even through her gloves. Elizabeth blushed and seemed as affected. Her hand lingered on his for just a moment too long until Mr. Gardiner approached.

Chapter 3

Georgiana was now perfectly convinced Elizabeth was the answer to the very prayer she made earlier in the day. Her brother was impressed with Elizabeth's intelligence; that was quite obvious. If his staring at her the entire evening was any clue, Georgiana hazarded a guess her brother was enraptured with Elizabeth's beauty as well.

Normally her brother was nearly as shy as she when meeting a new acquaintance and yet Elizabeth and the Gardiners worked their magic on both siblings. Neither sibling was nervous or reserved in their presence. Darcy even flattered and teased Elizabeth, something Georgiana knew him to never do with another lady.

She was glad Elizabeth first met her brother at the park and with a small group of strangers instead of at a crowded gathering in Hertfordshire, as he was certain to offend in such a place. A smile graced her face as she fell asleep. Her romantic heart had not been entirely crushed by her ill-advised foray of the summer. She was insensible to any obstacle between her brother and her new friend.

Darcy's sleep was not as contended. He was a man prone to reflection; it suited his fastidious nature. And this evening, he found his character wanting. He had told his sister, and it was true, he had always known birth did not make a person superior. But aside from displaying this in his choice of friends, he had been largely silent on the issue.

Darcy realized his actions were due to pride and vanity. He knew such opinions were not well accepted by the first circles of society and he was afraid if he should make his feelings known then his family name might be besmirched.

A lesser man might be resentful a woman was able to enlighten him so, but Darcy could only marvel that Elizabeth could do what his peers and tutors had not. He resolved to judge people by their actions and characters and not be prejudiced by their rank at all. It may prove to be a difficult lesson, but one worth the learning.

Darcy quickly realized Elizabeth had more to recommend her than just intelligence and wit. He determined her to be a devoted and loyal sister and delightfully genial. She was enchanting twirling a child while wearing muddied petticoats. Despite her protestations, she behaved the proper lady and he could not find her accomplishments wanting.

He recalled her words to her aunt about her lack of fortune and her family, and though the relations he met were respectable, even without knowing their background, they certainly could not further his situation in life.

Ah, there is the pride and vanity again. What do I need for more wealth or a higher standing in society? In vain have I struggled to find a companion of mind and spirits that met society's expectations of wealth and connections, and it will not do. I shall not condemn myself to loneliness to satisfy the opinions of others.

The only problem with his new resolve for a possible courtship with Miss Bennet was he had absolutely no idea how to go about it. The very thought kept him awake most of the night.

In Gracechurch Street Elizabeth reflected on the day and she could not help but smile. She found Miss Darcy quite agreeable and was pleased with her treatment from Mr. Darcy. She enjoyed he was neither intimidated by nor resentful of her intelligence and impertinence. She greatly looked forward to furthering the acquaintance. And while she noticed his eyes upon her frequently she could not suppose to be an object of admiration to so great a man. She was also not so vain as to fancy admiration to mean more than it did.

Elizabeth was perfectly convinced no sensible man should desire her for a wife. Five seasons in society had persuaded her of the truth of this sentiment. If she was dissatisfied with that answer more than usual and found it difficult to sleep, she cared not to investigate any deeper cause than the nerves she usually acquired before travelling home.

*****

The Darcy party was quite punctual and arrived at the Gardiner home a few minutes before nine. Darcy was pleased to see Elizabeth was prepared for their departure and did not keep them waiting. The Gardiner children, however, did.

As Elizabeth hugged her aunt farewell, Mrs. Gardiner remarked on the weather. "How warm it is for the first of October. I hope it will not affect your travels." She looked toward the sky. Unseasonable changes in temperature frequently brought storms but the day was cloudless.

"It has been unusually warm lately. What is it called again, Brother?"

"I have heard it called many things. St Martin's Summer, for St Martin's feast in November and St Luke's Summer for the corresponding feast in October. I think the most relevant one for now is St Michael's Little Summer, as we are only a few days past Michaelmas."

"How interesting! I have never heard it before!" Mrs. Gardiner replied.

"It is what the Welsh prefer to call it. I heard it called thus while attending to one of my estates, just outside the Welsh border in Shropshire. Many of the workers have a Welsh heritage."

"Mama! Mama! Tell him!" Michael was suddenly pulling on Mrs. Gardiner's skirts.

"What dear?"

"Tell Mr. Darcy I am not a saint, I'm an angel!" Michael demanded in all seriousness and all of the adults except Mr. Darcy broke out in laughter.

Seeing his confused face Elizabeth managed to explain between chuckles. "Michael is named after the archangel, as is his brother Gabriel. His sisters are named for their grandmothers who have passed. We have explained to him they are now angels in Heaven watching down on us. Incidentally, nearly everyone he knows is named for a passed relative. Only he is quite convinced he is an angel. I suppose he believes they cannot be punished."

Finally understanding the situation, Darcy chuckled. Elizabeth felt her heart rate increase when she saw his broad smile, complete with devastating dimples, again.

"And it is not summer. Miss Fields told us it is now Odd...odd...Oddum!" Michael grinned, immensely proud at remembering the unusual sounding word.

"Oddum?" Darcy paused, thinking over what word the little one was attempting to pronounce.

"Oh, Autumn. Yes, it is, Master Michael. But sometimes the weather acts differently than we expect and we come up with silly names for it. It has been so warm it is like a little summer and since it is close to St Michael's feast day we have come up with the name St Michael's Little Summer. Do you think you can share your name with the weather?"

"Yes, sir! Angels always share." Michael beamed again.

Mrs. Gardiner felt it best to prod Michael along while he proved compliant. Another quick farewell to Mr. and Mrs.

Gardiner and the Darcy carriage was finally headed towards Hertfordshire.

*****

Inside the carriage Elizabeth grinned at her companions. "Thank you again, Mr. Darcy and Miss Darcy for conveying me to Longbourn in your carriage. I apologize for Michael delaying us; I am his godmother and he is quite attached to me. I admit he has a special place in my heart, though I dearly love them all."

"I am very pleased to have you ride with us, Miss Bennet. It was no trouble at all to properly farewell the children. They are simply adorable." Georgiana replied.

"And it is no wonder the lad enjoys your company, you seem perfectly natural with them." *Yes, you are made to have a brood of children. I must stop this ridiculous thinking! I barely know her!*

"Thank you both. You do well with them too, sir."

Darcy blushed but Georgiana replied for him. "William has raised me almost entirely on his own. My mother died shortly after my birth. Father grieved for her and though he was always kind, he could withdraw from us at times.

"Father did not send William to school and instead he stayed at home with tutors and although I had my nurse and my governess, it was William that showed me affection. Once at University he was forever arranging to take exams early with his professors so he might have more time to visit with me."

Darcy blushed and Georgiana paused for a moment. Elizabeth saw a shadow fall across their eyes, remembering some unpleasantness. "Father died five years ago and William and our cousin are now my guardians. William is very good with children."

Elizabeth wondered at why there was no mentioning of help from female relatives. Wanting to lighten the mood and bring a smile to her new friends, Elizabeth asked, "Miss Darcy, would it be too forward to ask you to call me Elizabeth or Lizzy? And Mr. Darcy you must begin to call me Miss

Elizabeth, as my eldest sister is Miss Bennet."

Darcy could not contain his smile and Elizabeth felt her heart rate increase again. That is happening all too frequently. I am either no better than silly Lydia or should speak with the apothecary.

"I would love that, Elizabeth. And you must call me Georgiana." She seemed grateful for the change of topic. "I believe I heard you say last night that you have four sisters? I have always desired a sister."

Elizabeth laughed. "They are not always blessings, I assure you. One is always taking a gown or an accessory. I have often wished for a brother instead! But, yes I do have four sisters."

"And what are they like? Do they all play pianoforte and sing as you?"

Elizabeth smiled at Georgiana's enthusiasm and hoped again the Darcys could withstand her family's silliness.

"Jane is very beautiful and serene. She sees only the best in everyone, and unlike my cousin Michael, one could truly mistake her for an angel. Jane prefers riding to the pianoforte but my sister Mary enjoys playing very much. She dedicates many hours to practicing. I fear she is sometimes a bit lost amongst us and is given to the unsociable practice of reading even in the presence of others.

"Kitty and Lydia are quite silly young things. It might be indelicate of me to say this of my own family, and to new friends, but you will see it soon enough. They need a stronger hand but my father was raised in a very strict household and is convinced that does more harm than good."

She let out an exasperated sigh. "My mother's family had unfortunate experiences with their governesses and so we have never had one, and though my father has encouraged all of us to read and we have had all the masters that are necessary, my youngest sisters have chosen idleness and gossip as their main means of employment. But whatever their faults, I do love them dearly. They are young yet and I hope can improve with time."

Georgiana and Darcy shared a look which Elizabeth could not decipher and she held her breath, preparing for the worst.

"Lizzy, we know firsthand how difficult it is to find the right balance of authority and liberalness. It is a trying age, to be sure. I am certain with a sister such as you to guide them they cannot be so very bad. But you will find the Darcys are a loyal bunch. You have earned our friendship and you shall not lose it due to your family."

Stifling a giggle she added, "We are still friends with Mr. Bingley even though it means we both must suffer Miss Bingley's insincere flattery and attentions."

Elizabeth grinned at the picture painted. "Put that way, I understand perfectly!"

The occupants of the carriage decided it best to attempt some rest until they changed horses. In actuality the only person to find slumber was Mrs. Annesley. Georgiana, though knowing Elizabeth to be very kind, worried her new friend would think less of her if she knew of her past.

Elizabeth wondered at the silent conversation the siblings had earlier. She sensed Georgiana's words held a personal meaning for the two but knew it was too early in the acquaintance to inquire. She teetered between accepting Georgiana's words of loyalty and knowing her family would certainly test it.

Elizabeth was happy her new friends had met some of the family of which she need not blush. She attempted to remain hopeful the Darcys might not be offended by the silly exuberance of her mother and sisters or the indolence of her father.

Darcy spent more time reflecting on the further depths of Elizabeth's character she had revealed. *It is easy to judge but what are the reasons for a person's actions?*

Georgiana felt lonely, had been misguided and was handicapped by youth. Yet some would condemn her without knowing the story. Miss Elizabeth would never; she would see the truth and take Georgiana's wounded heart under her wing. Likewise, her family has its reasons for their own failures. We are, none of us, perfect.

*****

Georgiana and Mrs. Annesley were able to sleep after their scheduled stop. Darcy took advantage of the relative privacy. "Miss Elizabeth," he began, "I believe you promised me a debate."

She grinned at him. "Indeed, sir! Well, I will allow you to choose the subject then."

"I have been accustomed to ladies going first."

"And I have been accustomed to allowing those at the disadvantage to lead."

Darcy raised his eyebrows, "You perceive I am at the disadvantage? Even after knowing I out ranked your father?"

"I am confident, sir. I have found gentlemen always hold back when competing against a woman. I am convinced it is because when they lose to me they can then falsely congratulate themselves on not performing to their best ability and pretend to be able to keep their pride."

Darcy laughed at the image she created. "I can see you will be stubborn about this so I shall humour you. Your words just now have decided the topic for me. Let us debate faults and virtues."

"And shall you list yours, Mr. Darcy?"

"It is not for me to consider my virtues but I can list my faults well enough, I believe."

"You find yourself blind to your goodness but exceptionally aware of your flaws? That is rather singular. Most suffer from a conceited opinion of self-worth."

"I am not self-deprecating but I do enjoy the study of philosophy and theology and believe in meditating on my character. I had previously thought my greatest fault was an implacable resentment; my good opinion once lost is lost forever. However, I have recently realized I am guilty of pride and vanity as well."

"You did not list obstinacy as a fault, sir."

Darcy smiled, "I think you begin to understand me. I consider it more of a virtue, in my case."

"I wonder if you mean obstinacy or conviction. Are you so reckless as to adhere to your opinion out of obstinacy once your conviction is gone?"

"On occasion as a master I have had to face a decision in which I held no overwhelming certainty in my choice. To waver when a matter must be decided upon is to mark it for failure. I would rather remain steadfast in my previously made plans, even if I am not perfectly convinced of their correctness, than to sit in indecisiveness."

"As a leader of men I see that would be a necessary quality. If you are later convinced that your prior belief was incorrect, do you make amends?"

"Of course. I am guilty of pride and vanity, but not arrogance and conceit. As master it might wound my pride to admit an error but it would be dangerous to lose the respect of my servants and tenants out of conceit."

"As I see it your virtues then are wisdom, benevolence and steadfastness. I would think now, sir, it is time to evaluate my own faults."

"Miss Elizabeth, you are without fault, I am perfectly convinced." He spoke with all seriousness but she did not perceive it.

Laughing merrily Elizabeth replied, "I did not know you could tease, sir! Without fault, indeed! Last evening I spoke on many of them. I am impertinent and outspoken and you may infer I am perhaps too self-assured in my opinions."

"I stand by my statements of last night; I do not find you impertinent. I admire the liveliness of your mind and I find myself quite sick of deference."

Elizabeth blushed and before she could reply Georgiana awoke then and the threesome conversed about their favourite activities.

*****

"As much as I love reading and my excursions, I admit to be fond of dancing as well. We have frequent assemblies in

Meryton." Elizabeth's eyes shone in merriment.

Georgiana laughed. "You shall find William prefers to stand about by himself."

"I have not the talent which some people possess of conversing easily with those I have never seen before." Darcy explained.

"Perhaps that may be remedied by practice."

Darcy smiled and conceded, "Perhaps you are correct, Miss Elizabeth. And I shall ask the honour of a set with you at the next ball."

Elizabeth arched an eyebrow and responded. "I am afraid, sir, my dance card is already nearly full. I have a standing arrangement with many of my old friends of the neighbourhood and have only the fourth and last sets available."

Without a moment's hesitation Darcy knew he wanted to end any evening in the company of Elizabeth and applied for the last set. He desired to ask for a similar arrangement for himself but felt their acquaintance too new.

Elizabeth accepted with alacrity and then explained the next assembly was scheduled for the morrow. Darcy found he had never looked forward to a dance more. The conversation drifted towards literature and plays until they at last passed the gates of Longbourn.

Mercifully, only Mr. Bennet was home and able to greet the Darcys. Elizabeth was happy to avoid her mother's effusions upon the kindness of the Darcys and cost of their carriage- all wasted on the ungrateful Elizabeth.

Georgiana was disappointed to not meet the other Bennet ladies but hoped to call on them tomorrow. She was eager for more friends and any means of escaping Caroline Bingley.

Darcy was scarcely less eager to escape Miss Bingley, though his attraction to Longbourn centred on one particular Bennet lady.

Chapter 4

The morning after his arrival in Hertfordshire found Darcy awake early and the first in the breakfast room. He hoped Georgiana would be down soon so they might go on a walk. They did not have a private moment together the night before so unfortunately no definite plans had been made.

Darcy knew Caroline would try to invite herself or create a deterrent for his plans if she knew of them. Last night, when she was not flattering him or Georgiana, she was disparaging the Bennet family. She described the unfortunate behaviour of the younger sisters, the vulgarity of the mother and the poor connections. She claimed to hold the eldest Miss Bennet as a friend but Darcy knew the insincerity of Miss Bingley's affections. She never missed a moment to laugh at or belittle her friends in Town.

When Caroline began to censure Elizabeth he was certain she was being at the very least overly critical of the others, and entirely wrong about Elizabeth. Though it would be unwise to approve or disapprove before meeting the family, Darcy was of a mind to consider them harmless.

Just as Darcy was very strongly considering leaving on his own for his exercise, not caring to question his reasons, Bingley entered the breakfast room.

"Good morning, Darcy. I hope you do not have plans this morning. I thought you and Miss Darcy should like to call upon the Bennets with me." Darcy attempted to hide his smile with his coffee cup.

"Very well, Bingley. I am sure Georgiana should like the scheme. She was disappointed to not meet the other Bennet ladies yesterday."

"Darcy," Bingley began but paused clearly trying to find the best words. "I know Caroline has said much of the Bennet family, but you have already met Miss Elizabeth, so you must know how wrong my sister is. She does not allow for the differences between Town and country or of temper and disposition. I know you are uncomfortable in society and dislike displays of the ridiculous and generally do not care if others find you arrogant, but..."

"Say no more, Bingley, I perfectly understand."

"You do? You are not offended at what I have said?"

"I have recently been persuaded to practice conversation with strangers."

"Well, that is..." Bingley trailed off, seemingly uncomfortable with the notion of Darcy admitting to any sort of weakness or deficiency.

"Shall we depart in two hours then?" The conversation then turned to how Bingley was finding the estate and the country.

*****

Mr. Bingley and the Darcys arrived at Longbourn after being delayed by Miss Bingley only momentarily. Mrs. Annesley stayed behind to rest after so much travel in such a short time. Darcy was surprised at Bingley's resolve to leave as his friend typically fell easily to his sister's manipulations. Darcy surmised there must be an 'angel' in residence at Longbourn to provide the motivation.

Nary a second after the introductions Mrs. Bennet began, "Oh, you do us a great honour Mr. Darcy in bringing Lizzy home to us. I see the rumours of your wealth must be true. What a fine carriage!"

Seeing she would not gain a response from him she turned to his sister. "And Miss Darcy, the silk of your gown!"

Five years in London society taught Darcy to quickly see the mercenary glint in Mrs. Bennet's eyes.

He internally cringed for a moment before catching her next words, "Yes, Miss Darcy you will find my Lydia is lively company. She is quite the favourite among her sisters. With only a much older brother you must be in want of a sister."

Is Mrs. Bennet trying to match me with that— that child laughing too loudly in the corner?

"You enjoy the pianoforte, do you? Lydia does not favour practicing; if she did she would be a true proficient. That is why she is favoured at all the balls; she is greatly skilled in dancing." Darcy could hardly contain his laughter when he heard words alarmingly similar to his aunt, Lady Catherine de Bourgh's. He realized Mrs. Bennet was indeed no worse than his own embarrassing family. His disgust turned to amusement just as Mr. Bennet, who witnessed the transformation, walked in the room.

After his introduction, the older gentleman began, "Mr. Fitzwilliam Darcy, it is a pleasure to finally meet you, sir. I have heard of your debating skills but I can clearly see you share my mixture of quick parts, reserve and sarcastic humour."

Darcy heartily laughed at the picture of himself and quickly realized he could do to learn from Mr. Bennet's ability to manage the situation of boisterous Bennet women.

"Mr. Bennet, a pleasure to meet you, sir! I gather you are a studier of character like your daughter, then."

"I see you have survived your time with Elizabeth. May I presume she engaged you in battle sir?"

"Yes, I must give my compliments to you for teaching her so well!" Elizabeth overheard and blushed.

"Lizzy has more of a quickness to her than my other daughters, you shall find. I wish I could take all the credit but she has a natural desire to learn."

Before Darcy could reply he was interrupted by Mrs. Bennet, "Lizzy is not a bit better than the others; and I am sure she is not half so handsome as Jane, nor half so good-humoured as Lydia. But you are always giving her the preference."

Elizabeth trembled lest her mother should be exposing herself again. She longed to speak but could think of nothing to say.

After a short silence Mrs. Bennet began again, "The weather is so warm for October, and Mr. and Miss Darcy have not seen the grounds. Lydia, I am sure they would delight in the wilderness."

Casting another glance about the room she added, "Perhaps Mr. Bingley and Jane could be persuaded to join you."

"Mama, I wanted to walk to town to see if Mr. Denny has returned in time for the

Assembly. Miss Darcy, you should come with me, for we always meet with officers and have a merry time!"

Darcy's head snapped to attention at her words but before he could utter his vehemence at the plan Elizabeth was roused to speak at last.

"I am sure Miss Darcy is tired from her travels yesterday. I would be happy to escort her and Mr. Darcy in the garden while you and Kitty walk to town."

*****

Once outside Elizabeth began, "Georgiana, Mr. Darcy, I apologize for my family. I failed to warn you of my mother yesterday. I had hoped she would have been more distracted by," she glanced at Jane and Mr. Bingley conversing ahead of them, "other matters.

"It does not excuse her behaviour, but our estate is entailed upon a cousin. His father was very mean spirited and she fears the son could carry the same grudge against my father. At any rate, with no son, she is unusually anxious about our future and tenacious about matchmaking where her daughters are concerned. Pray, take no heed to her, she is discouraged easily enough."

Darcy looked at her earnestly and sought to ease her discomfort. "We all have peculiar relatives, Miss Elizabeth, and neither her concerns nor her actions are particularly unique or offensive."

He was speaking the truth. Mrs. Bennet might be annoying and vulgar but he doubted her scheming enough to manipulate compromising scenarios as he had been made a target of by others.

"You are too kind, sir." The threesome walked in silence for a moment until Mr. Bingley called Darcy's attention ahead.

Georgiana seized upon the privacy. She turned to Elizabeth and asked, "Lizzy, have you ever been in love?"

Elizabeth was a bit taken aback by the question but realized Georgiana likely had no other young ladies to speak to on those sorts of subjects. With sisterly affection she answered, "No, Georgiana, I have not. I have admired a few gentlemen but never felt the lasting affection of love."

"How can you say for sure you did not?"

"Well, I realized my feelings were based upon the excitement of attention. The gentlemen did not inspire deeper feelings and upon reflection of their character they were found wanting.

"The best kind of love grows from a steady friendship, supported by respect and esteem. One should feel safe and cherished in a unique way not experienced in other relationships. Does that make sense?"

"I think so. And how are you sure love is returned?"

"Well, these are things I have not truly experienced but I have noticed love is selfless. A person who is in love will be attuned to their beloved's desires. What would be a sacrifice for themselves will give them delight, if it pleases their beloved."

"I see. Thank you, Lizzy. And you have truly never been in love? You are too beautiful!"

Elizabeth laughed. "You really must stop saying so, for you are feeding my vanity. Now, I will answer your question. Truly I have never been in love before. Besides, my appearance has nothing to do with if I have been in love and it certainly has done nothing to inspire love in others. Any attraction gentlemen have felt for me dies when they see Jane, or even before if I speak too freely."

"Lizzy, how can you not see how beautiful and wonderful you are?"

"I am not afflicted with false modesty when I say you shall see I pale in comparison to Jane. My temperament is not as sweet as hers, nor is it as lively as Lydia's.

"You will easily see I am meant to be the spinster friend to all the gentlemen of Hertfordshire; all the more for them to become closer to Jane. My mother, for all her faults, is quite correct in her assessment of my marital prospects, even if she lacks tact in how it is presented."

Trying to not display her sadness at feeling so unaccepted she turned the subject back towards Georgiana, "Why do you ask all these questions?"

"I thought I had been in love and believed he loved me, but then I later learned he most decidedly did not love me. But I see from your examples I was never truly in love either. I have wanted to ask someone so I could be sure next time."

"Yes, this is a subject that one would want to ask a lady and not a brother one looks to almost as a father."

"Exactly. Though, I believe he is gaining experience in matters of the heart." They had turned just then and espied Mr. Darcy waiting for them and so no reply could be made.

Elizabeth found it difficult to account for the sinking in her heart she felt at Georgiana's last words.

It is a wonder a man as handsome, wealthy, intelligent and kind as he is still unattached in the first place. Yes, some great lady has rightly earned his admiration. I knew it must be so and I have no right to repine. I am not the sort of woman he would want.

The ladies did not know Mr. Darcy had been able to hear most of their conversation.

She is helping Georgiana so much. But has her heart truly never been touched? What is wrong with the men in Hertfordshire? Can they not see her worth? How dare they use her just to meet her sister!

Bingley announced the carriage had been called for; each member was so distracted by their own thoughts none noticed the subdued farewell between Darcy and Elizabeth.

*****

In Meryton Kitty and Lydia were just giving up the purpose of their travels when Mr. Denny stepped out from a shop with an officer they had not met before. The man had all the best part of beauty, a fine countenance, a good figure and very pleasing address. Lydia made headlong for them.

"No, Lydia we do not have time. Mama wants you to have enough time to dress to impress Mr. Darcy tonight. She thinks Miss Darcy was quite taken with you and would welcome you as a sister. Although, I think they both prefer Lizzy."

"La! Why would I want a dull man like Mr. Darcy?" She grabbed Kitty by the hand and launched her the last few feet to the gentlemen.

"Mr. Denny! We had come into to town just to inquire after you!"

"As you see, Miss Lydia, I have returned in time to claim a set with you this evening!" He spoke to Lydia but her attention was already captured by his friend.

"Of course! What fun we shall have! And who is your friend?" Lydia fluttered her eyelashes coquettishly.

"Allow me to introduce Lieutenant George Wickham. Wickham, these fine ladies are Miss Catherine Bennet and Miss Lydia Bennet."

George Wickham turned his most charming smile upon the young ladies. He had overheard their conversation and believed Hertfordshire would prove a most fruitful endeavour.

*****

The Assembly started pleasant enough. Darcy did not dance the early dances and chose instead to acquaint himself with some of the local gentlemen, carefully reminding himself of Elizabeth's admonishment. As he conversed he was ever aware of her position on the dance floor, and her partner. Although Elizabeth claimed the gentlemen were only interested in friendship from her, Darcy believed he perceived some partiality from one or two.

He realized it might be ungentlemanly but he desired to send a clear message to the community. He would dance with no one outside his party this evening but Elizabeth. Seeing her in the company of other men, he decided he would speak with her father very soon about a courtship. Darcy was so involved in his meditations and the exhausting practice of speaking with strangers that he missed many details of the evening.

Elizabeth was mortified. Upon the Netherfield party's arrival Mrs. Bennet had alternately insulted Mr. Darcy for not bringing Georgiana and then sickeningly flattered him and tried to bring Lydia to his notice once more. He briefly greeted them and then all but ran towards a corner to speak with some gentlemen.

As the evening wore on she saw his disapproval every time he glanced upon her. Lydia and Kitty flirted loudly and outrageously. Clearly any respect he felt for her was sinking, everything must sink under such a proof of family weakness. She could neither wonder nor condemn. She now feared her dance with him.

Lost in these unhappy thoughts, Lydia and George Wickham came upon her.

"Lizzy! You have not met Mr. Wickham yet! He recently joined the Militia. Isn't he just dashing in a red coat?" Lydia giggled.

"I am pleased to meet you, Miss Elizabeth. Could I have the honour of your next available set?"

Elizabeth politely acquiesced, allowing him her only open set, which proved to be next.

Once dancing Wickham began his campaign, "Your sisters tell me you are newly acquainted with Mr. Darcy of Pemberley."

"Yes, sir. We met in Town just before he intended to travel here to visit his friend. Do you know him?"

"Oh, yes. We grew up on the same estate. My father was his father's steward and we were the closest companions in our youth. I was a favourite of his father. The current Mr. Darcy and I have drifted apart after he took over his estate and I completed university."

"How fortunate to meet again, then."

"I am unsure if he would count it as fortunate. When last we met we had a terrible disagreement."

"Sir, I wonder…"

"Forgive me, I know I must sound forward, but the disagreement was of a nature that I cannot help but worry for any young lady who makes his acquaintance."

Elizabeth gasped at his words, "Surely not, sir. He is very gentleman-like." Mr. Darcy a rake?

"He can please where he chooses. And I do not mean to imply anything too sinister. But you see he is engaged to marry his cousin. Our last disagreement was due to him desiring to break apart a lady's engagement to keep her affections for himself. I would not wish to see you or your sisters' affections trifled with when he can have no intentions as he is destined for another."

Elizabeth moved through the remaining paces of the dance in a daze and did not register Wickham's knowing smirk. Seeking to settle herself she made her way to the punch table, only to be accosted by Miss Bingley.

"Miss Eliza! So nice to see you after your banishment to London! I hear you have already met Mr. Darcy and his sister and even had the audacity to importune on them for a ride to Longbourn. While I am sure those sorts of plots work well on the men of the country, you must see Mr. Darcy will not be deceived by your charms.

"He needs a woman of class and breeding with beauty and wealth. Really, Eliza, you would do better to try to gain the attention of one of these officers. Just follow your sisters. They quite excel in the art." Before Elizabeth could even reply the lady fled with a great rustling of garish skirts.

Elizabeth determined that the revelations of the evening should not disturb her. She had always known she could never attract any worthy man and never once assumed Mr. Darcy would think of her. But the pounding in her head could not be ignored. Now feeling truly ill she begged her mother to call the carriage. Accompanied by her sister Mary, she slipped out of the assembly hall. She longed for solitude and her bed.

Chapter 5

George Wickham hid in the shadows of the ballroom, the last thing he needed was to be seen by one of those ridiculous Bennet girls before he intended. At last he saw Darcy enter. Instead of eschewing conversation with the others in attendance, and inadvertently giving offence, the man was actually speaking to the country gentlemen!

Wickham could not understand Darcy's departure from his usual behaviour, until the first set began. Darcy's attention seemed to constantly be drawn towards a lively young lady who was quite attractive but not a remarkable beauty.

He supposed Darcy was attempting to court the woman and her neighbours' good opinion. Wickham had been hesitant to believe the gossip he heard from the Bennet sisters, that his old pal Darcy was actually showing a preference for a lady. Wickham was well acquainted with discerning the way other men looked at ladies, in an attempt to avoid disputes when beginning his conquests, and he could easily see Darcy was besotted.

Darcy's choice surprised Wickham, as the handsomest woman in the room was dancing with Darcy's long-time friend, Bingley. Wickham truly had no idea what features might attract Darcy in a woman, as he had never seen the man show partiality for one before this night. It surprised him that a man who could have anyone and anything did not seek greater beauty or wealth. Where was the man's pride?

Of course, Wickham knew Darcy's pride was familial, rather than due to this wealth and consequence. He would do anything but shame the Darcy name. A fact Wickham constantly took advantage of from childhood to present day. Still, Wickham knew his former friend was expected to make a great match from the first circles of London society to a woman of grace and wealth, with great beauty and connections. The animated little brunette held none of those attractions.

When Wickham saw the look of jealousy in Darcy's eyes repeatedly through the first few sets, he knew his plot would succeed. Wickham knew that expression on

Darcy's face well. It was often there after Darcy would find Wickham enjoying the attentions of old Mr. Darcy.

All Wickham needed was an introduction to Darcy's lady. He fervently hoped this was the 'Lizzy' he heard the Bennet girls speak of earlier. The youngest Bennet sister would perform all her parts admirably, he had no doubt at all.

*****

Caroline Bingley fumed. Darcy had not pre-arranged a set with her and then she learned Eliza Bennet had made a move on her Mr. Darcy. His visit to this God forsaken place was supposed to prove she was perfect for the role of mistress of Pemberley. Compared to these country chits, Caroline would show her superior fashion, taste, beauty and hostessing skills.

The evening started out poorly enough, by her estimation, but then she noticed Darcy was actually mingling with the tasteless and loud nobodies when he would not deign to speak at the most elegant balls in Town. She could not account for the change in his demeanour.

When she noticed his eyes darting to seek out Eliza Bennet, nearly nonstop, her anger grew. She hoped he was just watching for amusement, after all, he did not look particularly pleased. She would rescue him from this inane company.

Just before calling out to him she saw her brother approach, "Come, Darcy, I must see you dancing."

"I certainly shall not. You know how I detest it unless I am particularly acquainted with my partner. Am I not doing well enough by speaking with the gentlemen?"

"I dare say, I have never seen you so approachable, but you had much better dance. I have never seen so many pretty girls in my life. Several of them uncommonly pretty. I can introduce you to whichever you like."

"As it happens, I have already made an arrangement with the only woman in the room I care to join."

"You only arrived yesterday! And I have not seen you speak to a lady this evening. The only ones you have met at all are the Bennet sisters. Come man, which is it?"

"Miss Elizabeth Bennet."

"Miss Elizabeth! I am all astonishment. That must have been some carriage ride indeed to feel 'particularly acquainted.'" Bingley could not help but tease.

Darcy would not be baited, however, and resolutely told Bingley to return to his partner. "Aside from dancing with Miss Elizabeth and fulfilling my duty with your sisters, I am quite content to converse with the gentlemen."

Caroline's control over her rage evaporated. She seized her opportunity when she saw Elizabeth head towards the punch table.

*****

When Darcy entered the Assembly hall he had little hopes of enjoying anything but his dance with Elizabeth. He was determined, however, to please her by showing he respected her opinions and chastisement, no matter how uncomfortable he felt.

At first he even entertained the notion of standing up with another lady or two, breaking his long held standard of not dancing with a stranger. When he noticed the looks of admiration she received from her dance partners, Darcy found he could not dance with another.

By the third set he had even resolved to imitate Bingley, who had plans to dance twice with Jane, and ask Elizabeth for her last remaining set. He began to move in her direction when he was accosted by Sir William Lucas.

"Do you not find dancing a very enjoyable exercise, sir?"

The old Darcy would have coldly tried to deter this man from his meaningless small talk, but Darcy sacrificed his comfort to be civil. "Truthfully, I much prefer conversation. I dislike being on display, but find others quite enjoy it."

"It is the mark of every great society, I am sure."

Darcy bit back a sarcastic remark. "You must be correct, sir."

"You must often attend the balls at St. James Place."

In actuality Darcy only attended when forced by familial obligation. "I go but rarely, sir."

Sir William, for all of his superciliousness realized Darcy would not prove conversant on the subject. "You have a house in Town?"

Darcy allowed it to be so and Sir William continued for some time on his determining Town unsuitable for Lady Lucas's health. He then raised the topic of his daughter, Charlotte, and her recent marriage to a Mr. Collins. The very one Darcy overheard Elizabeth speak of in the park and who had recently received a living from Lady Catherine de Bourgh.

Sir William asked if Darcy knew of the great lady. Darcy realized he should deny any acquaintance with the lady in an interest to reach Elizabeth before the next set began. Although disguise of every sort was his abhorrence, he was just determining to do so when he saw an officer approach Elizabeth and they made for the dance floor.

Realizing that he lost the dance and believing that she was too sensible to be attracted to an officer, undoubtedly of paltry means, he turned his attention back to Sir William, without ever seeing the officer's face.

*****

When Sir William was, at long last, called off on some matter, Darcy was reminded of his duty to Bingley's sisters. During his set with Mrs. Hurst he noticed that he could not espy Elizabeth. Growing concerned he beseeched Bingley to enquire intelligence from Miss Bennet. Darcy was excessively disappointed when he learned Elizabeth felt ill and had already left. Dark thoughts flooded his mind.

Did she leave because she did not want to dance with me? If she could not welcome the attentions of the gentlemen she has known all of her life, who all seem affable, amiable and intelligent, why should she enjoy mine?

His mind raced over their recent encounters for some indication she had felt truly affronted or indifferent towards him. Just then, Miss Bingley approached and Darcy felt he had no alternative but to ask her for the next set.

Once the dancing began, the lady bravely began. "I was surprised to hear of your acquaintance with Miss Eliza Bennet. I wonder you did not say a thing last night. You must have been very weary from your journey in such tedious company."

"On the contrary, we enjoyed lively conversation and debate."

"Debate? What could the impertinent girl have been thinking? To dare think her opinion equal to your own!"

"I dare say her opinion is, and even better informed in some cases."

"I wonder how you tolerate her, or allow dear Georgiana near her and those sisters. The Bennet girls are nothing more than mercenary flirts. Just see how the eldest has thrown herself at Charles this evening."

"Miss Bingley," Darcy replied coldly, "you know as well as I, a lady does not choose her partner." He hoped she would understand he found her behaviour lacking but she did not seem to notice so he continued.

"If Miss Bennet is frequently seen in Bingley's company it is from his desire. I see nothing in her countenance which could be seen as either mercenary or flirtatious."

He paused to allow the next words prominence, "And I assure you, I am well acquainted with both."

Miss Bingley was not to be deterred. "So you believe her indifferent?"

"I believe she is acting as a lady should, though my opinion is of no matter."

"How can you say that? She will be the ruin of Charles. Her family has a total want of propriety, no fortune and no connections. I am convinced Miss Eliza has designs on you. I had to warn her away just earlier this evening."

"What did you say?" Darcy's jaw was clenched tightly.

"I simply reminded her of your need for a wife of good breeding, poise, wealth and connections."

"I have no need for you to defend my business. I shall know how to act." Caroline Bingley left the dance feeling confident Darcy had been reminded of Elizabeth's place and was safe for her clutches alone.

Rather than give offence due to his foul mood, Darcy called for his carriage and arranged for it to return to convey the remainder of the Netherfield Party home later. He quickly realized that Elizabeth must feel as though he found her wanting and might even feel her affections trifled with.

I will count myself fortunate if she will want to speak with me again after being so abused by my acquaintances.

Despite his misgivings, before falling into a fitful sleep he had determined to walk out early in the morning with every hope of encountering Elizabeth alone.

*****

At Longbourn Elizabeth's headache did not lessen. Before she finally managed to fall asleep Elizabeth felt only disappointment. Mr. Darcy had been too good to be true. Never before had she met a man with the intelligence and character she could truly esteem. Never before had she felt so accepted and respected.

She was only too sensible to his position in life and while she thought she took care to not allow herself fanciful thoughts, she realized her heart had betrayed her.

Early the next morning Elizabeth awoke before sunrise, but with no headache. She determined the matter required another perusal when she was not quite so affected. She left the house to climb Oakham Mount just as the first rays of sun emerged. When she reached the peak, she allowed herself time to meditate on her concerns with her eyes closed and feeling the warmth of the sun.

First, she considered Mr. Wickham's testimony. She must allow that she did not truly know Mr. Darcy very well; theirs had been a very brief acquaintance. She next conceded she did not know Wickham at all. She recalled the man mentioned not meeting with Mr. Darcy for many years and yet seemed too ready to slander him. Perhaps Darcy had changed and should be allowed to prove himself before being charged for old ways.

She shook her head at the faulty thought, it sounded too much like Jane. She did believe people could alter their behaviour, but only with sufficient motivation. If Mr. Darcy had once been a rake, he most likely would continue to be. He had either always been good or never good.

She thought again on the length of time Wickham mentioned. If Mr. Darcy had been engaged all those years ago then why was he still unmarried? Perhaps he still held hope to somehow dissolve the betrothal and marry the other lady? But Wickham implied Darcy felt no lasting affection for the woman in question and instead believed Darcy dangerous to any lady. Then why should he not be married? Why should he single Elizabeth out?

Additionally, the attention was given in full view of his younger sister and her family. She began to surmise Wickham was spinning tales, but could not quite piece together why.

Elizabeth then turned her mind to Miss Bingley's words. It took less time to puzzle out her words only reflected her feelings of Elizabeth as a rival. Most irksome was that Caroline had somehow known all of Elizabeth's sore spots and she played right into Caroline's plan.

There was quite a bit of truth in her words, though. Darcy would be expected to marry a woman from London high society. Elizabeth knew her beauty was easily withstood and she had no fortune or connections and meagre accomplishments. She simply could not compete on those levels with the London ladies.

Why should Caroline feel so threatened? Elizabeth considered Darcy's actions at the Assembly. He mingled with the gentlemen but seemed to glare at her. Yet, if he was looking at her in disapproval, in light of her family's behaviour, then why should Caroline worry at all?

Suddenly, Darcy's words flooded her memory. He had found her intelligent, charming and even accomplished. He called her refreshing and stated he did not like deference. When he met Jane, he did not even spare her beauty a glance, preferring to gaze at Elizabeth. He was all kindness in the face of her mother's antics and even alluded to embarrassing family of his own. His sister decreed him loyal and even Elizabeth declared him constant. If she had earned his admiration, she would not lose it.

She began to hope as she realized that if Mr. Darcy had truly desired a match like Caroline described then he could have easily married his cousin, Caroline or any other London lady by now. Perhaps he wanted a love match.

The only question remaining in Elizabeth's mind was if she would welcome his attentions. She laughed to herself at the thought. No, there was no question at all! Without intentional thought she had been answering that question all along. She had truly, finally, met a man who inspired her respect and admiration and never before had she so earnestly desired its reciprocation. Elizabeth realized Wickham and Caroline had meant to frighten her, but her courage always rose with every attempt at intimidation.

*****

She did not hear Darcy's footsteps as he paused to watch her. Her eyes had been closed. Despite the bonnet she wore, he could see some of her beautiful face bathed in the warm beams of the sun. He was fascinated by the variety of emotions which passed over her and was entirely enchanted by her laugh, pleased to see she was well.

Suddenly she opened her eyes and saw the earnest expression on his face, "Mr. Darcy!"

He bowed and smiled, "Miss Bennet."

They stood facing each other, both searching for some sign. Finally Darcy asked, "I heard you were ill last evening. Are you feeling better?"

"Yes, I thank you. Are you well this morning?"

"Yes, quite." Another silence ensued. "I was very sorry to miss our dance last night."

"Forgive me, I was very unwell."

"I am glad to see you recovered." He paused for a moment and then acted on impulse. He pulled off his hat and tossed it under a nearby tree.

Next he looked at Elizabeth intently and asked, "May I?"

Elizabeth was unsure what he meant, but could deny him nothing and merely nodded her consent.

He stepped closer and reached to untie the ribbons of her bonnet. She could scarcely breathe between his closeness and the intimacy of his actions. Darcy gently pulled the bonnet off and placed it next to his hat and then smiled broadly, "Much better. I can see your whole face and your lovely hair."

She blushed and he was charmed anew. He took her hand and bowed over it. "Miss Elizabeth, may I have the honour of this dance?"

She laughed, "I hear no music, sir."

"Do you not?" He began to hum the tune of a simple dance and was delighted when she joined in.

They went through several steps before he spoke again, "Shall we use this example of my obstinacy as a fault or a virtue, Miss Elizabeth?"

Elizabeth laughed again, "I suppose it depends on your level of conviction, sir."

He met her eyes, "I have never been more certain of anything."

"Then it must be a great virtue."

"What makes you think so?"

She gazed affectionately, "Because I am assured of your character, sir."

Darcy wished to alleviate her concerns on his affections and tentatively began. "I had a very...interesting conversation with Miss Bingley."

Elizabeth blushed, "As did I."

"I hope her words did not upset you."

"What will you think of my vanity when I admit they did? I am acutely aware of my folly in allowing Miss Bingley and Mr. Wickham's words to affect me."

Darcy could not believe his ears. "Pardon me, did you say Mr. Wickham? George Wickham?

"Yes." She could see he was distressed by the news. "He told me he was acquainted with you..."

"Miss Elizabeth, it is essential I escort you back to Longbourn immediately and then depart to Netherfield in all haste. It is probable I shall have to journey to London as well. I shall explain all when at Longbourn and I should like to meet with your father as well."

The urgency and alarm in his voice combined with his hands upon her made her head spin.

"Very well, sir. I shall not delay you for an instant." Darcy collected their hats before the pair walked briskly back to Longbourn.

They returned to the house just as the family had finished breakfast. Before Darcy could ask for his audience with Mr. Bennet, Mrs. Phillips was presented.

"Sister! I heard the most dreadful gossip concerning Lydia and Mr. Wickham!" She cried out, heedless of any who heard her.

Chapter 6

Mrs. Phillips, Elizabeth's maternal aunt, was even more vulgar than Mrs. Bennet. She did not shy away from repeating the most disgusting gossip and in the most outrageous language, even if it involved one of her nieces.

Nothing could be understood through Mrs. Bennet's shrieking, so she was promptly sent upstairs to be cared for by Jane and Kitty. Lydia was taken in her father's study with Mr. Bennet staring her down, Elizabeth crying silent tears and Mr. Darcy gazing out the window. Mary consoled herself with the accounts of fallen women illustrated by Dr Fordyce.

Although Lydia was resolute no compromise or liberties were taken, she affirmed that Mr. Wickham approached her on the balcony outside the assembly the previous night. She even attested to her innocence by naming Miss Bingley as a witness.

The gossip was decidedly worse and grew with each retelling, as gossip generally does. There was no doubt a marriage would have to be created between Wickham and Lydia, but honour would never induce him and the Bennets did not have the income for financial motivation. Darcy paced about the room, quickly deciding that he would settle Wickham's debts himself and find a new livelihood for him, away from Hertfordshire.

Darcy explained his history with Wickham to Mr. Bennet and Elizabeth. The scoundrel had always taken advantage of the Darcy family. From becoming the favourite of the late Mr. Darcy, spewing lies about a denied living about the current Mr. Darcy and even attempting to elope with Georgiana. He was also a known gamester and rake.

Darcy reasoned his need to offer assistance was due to his misguided loyalty to his father. In an effort to protect his family's reputation, he never exposed Wickham. Internally, he knew Wickham harmed the Bennet family because he saw Darcy's admiration for Elizabeth.

Mr. Bennet hesitated, but knew he could not refuse the aid. "You say Mr. Wickham is not very honourable, has debts all over, and is a practiced gamester. What sort of husband shall he make?" Mr. Bennet asked Darcy.

"I am afraid Miss Lydia's future life may not be very content." Mr. Bennet simply nodded in defeat.

Darcy was saddened to have to deliver any lady to the hands of such a man. Before exiting to take care of the matter with Wickham, Darcy took one long glance at Elizabeth. *I can never deserve her now. My admiration has only brought her pain and my pride allowed a villain loose upon her family.*

Elizabeth had watched as Darcy marched around the room. Her admiration grew tenfold when she heard his fixation on settling the matter. That he could conceive the fault lay with him instead of Wickham, Miss Bingley or even Lydia, was proof again of his superior character. *He is too just a gentleman to become brother to a man like Wickham.*

*****

George Wickham lingered in the officers' common areas certain Darcy would be searching him out soon. Events went even better than he had planned. He had not taken Miss Bingley and her jealousy into account in his plot. Her zealous desire to be Mrs. Darcy served Wickham quite well. The news of his supposed compromise of Lydia Bennet at the Assembly the previous night had travelled fast.

As the time grew late Wickham grew uneasy as he had expected Darcy hours earlier. At last his eyes alighted on a familiar frame entering the room and he schooled his features into calm disinterest.

"Wickham," Darcy growled out to the man.

"Darcy. What brings you here to this fine establishment?" Wickham returned.

"You know exactly what brings me here."

"My, I cannot seem to recall the last time you took such an eager interest in my affairs. Hmm…oh yes, it was last summer and you had just come to visit your sister."

Wickham delighted in baiting Darcy but knew better than to attempt to publicly smear Georgiana's name or admit to anything.

Darcy reddened and he unconsciously clinched his fists. "Wickham, do not test my patience."

Wickham could not resist going further. "Have you come to bring me news on your sister? Or perhaps just one you had hoped to make your sister?"

In Wickham's most extreme dreams his latest plot against Darcy would both cause the man extreme misery, as he could not marry Miss Elizabeth due to the scandal, and would also prove to be a profitable endeavour for him.

He realized this was unrealistic, the whole point of the marriage was to hush up the scandal, and happily settled upon the notion of marrying Miss Lydia for a sizeable sum. If the scandal was avoided then Darcy would marry Elizabeth, and Wickham was hopeful that he would be able to drain more from the Darcy coffers through a lifetime as brother to Darcy. It would also serve as quite a blow to his nemesis's pride and result in a suitable amount of revenge.

Darcy let out an uncharacteristic chuckle which alarmed Wickham greatly but the man was a true proficient at masking his thoughts. Darcy leaned forward and looked Wickham directly in the eye causing him to gulp and look away in uncertainty.

"I know your game, Wickham and you failed. It is true I have a care for the Bennet reputation and I am here to facilitate a marriage between Miss Lydia and yourself. But you will not find it very profitable. You see, since this summer my cousin, you remember Colonel Fitzwilliam, correct?" Darcy paused and Wickham merely nodded with a flash of fear in his eyes.

"Well, he has been reassigned to the war office in London and actually trained with Colonel Forster," Wickham closed his eyes realizing that all of his plans had turned to dust but Darcy continued. "A commission as an ensign has been bought for you in the _____ Regiment. You are to report to Newcastle by the 27th and should know the regiment has orders to depart for

Spain in the spring. You have seen the casualty rates, yes? You have no alternative and will not receive any financial inducement to marry Lydia. If you flee now then you shall be facing charges of desertion and my cousin will personally lead the chase."

Wickham paled as soon as Darcy mentioned Colonel Fitzwilliam, and as Darcy continued his narrative a bead of sweat began to inch down Wickham's charming face.

"What of Lydia? Surely the Bennets cannot wish for her to be a soldier's wife and for her to remain friendless in the North. How shall I support her on an ensign's pay? You would send your father's godson to battle? What if there are children left behind after my death?"

Darcy laughed again. "Miss Lydia shall stay at Longbourn. I shall settle some money on her, my solicitor is drawing up the documents for Mr. Bennet. It shall be in her name and for her discretion alone should you survive the war and she ever seek to join your household. For now, there will be no possibility for children by Miss Lydia."

He gave Wickham a hard look and Wickham entirely understood there would be no traditional wedding night. Darcy clearly did not desire any loose strings attached to Miss Lydia.

Additionally left unsaid was the fact that Wickham had several children by his conquests that he did not provide for and many more he had no knowledge of at all. Darcy and Wickham both knew that Wickham's interest in money to raise a family with was fabricated; his only interest was for himself.

*****

Darcy travelled to London to prepare Wickham's marriage to Lydia. He returned to Hertfordshire only to ensure the ceremony itself took place. Bingley was courting Jane Bennet and called constantly on Longbourn. Visiting Hertfordshire would mean spending too many hours either at Longbourn, torturing himself with the presence of Elizabeth, or at Netherfield with only the Hursts for company. Bingley had sent

Caroline to an aunt in Scarborough for her part in the scandal.

Darcy could not bear to see Elizabeth. He once thought he would marry her but now he knew she deserved better. What type of honourable gentleman had he been?

He knew what Wickham was! He dealt with Wickham many times over and yet he never considered the threat Wickham was to the greater public. To know that Wickham targeted Lydia Bennet because of Darcy's rumoured esteem for Elizabeth broke him.

In the past Wickham's schemes always involved maligning Darcy's name and reputation, but he firmly believed his character spoke for itself. Other than calling Wickham out, which was illegal and would jeopardize his family, Darcy had no recourse for Wickham's slander.

After the attempted elopement, Darcy desired to protect Georgiana's reputation. There was little he could do about the matter without enlightening the whole world to the affair. Was his sister's credit more important than that of innocent and respectable people everywhere? What of the tradesmen who offered Wickham credit? How many ladies were ruined at Wickham's hand? How many families were destroyed and left grieving? Darcy had never considered it. He had cared only for his family name and anything that might taint that made the cost too high. He let a villain run free.

Darcy had small hopes all of his efforts to ease Lydia's pain at becoming Mrs. Wickham, in addition to time, would lessen his affront to Elizabeth but she would not meet his eye and was not encouraging during his visit to the area. They were not placed near each other during dinner or at the same card table later. Even while refilling his coffee Elizabeth remained resolutely silent and preferred the company of a gaggle of women to him. Darcy could not blame her in the least.

Despite Mrs. Bennet's best attempts, the wedding breakfast was a subdued affair. There was much subterfuge involved in the handling of escorting Wickham and Lydia to London where she would stay with the Gardiners while Wickham continued on to Newcastle. To Darcy, Elizabeth appeared even less receptive to his attention during the attempted celebration.

When Darcy had met Elizabeth he realized quickly he was enchanted, bewitched even. On such a short acquaintance it was almost improper to ask for a courtship when he first intended, though his heart desired marriage even then.

After he left Netherfield, rather than face her rejection, he had much time to give the situation more thought. The fact was, he fell in love with her that day in the park as she twirled little Michael Gardiner around, with her petticoat six inches deep in mud. Before she even spoke, her mannerisms said much of her character. Surely their conversations detailed more illumination of character than many couples face in months of courting in a drawing room.

He thought back on Elizabeth's words to Georgiana about love. If asked the day before the Assembly he would have declared there was nothing on earth to motivate him to face George Wickham again. And yet when the news of his plot against the Bennet family fell, Darcy barely gave any thought at all to dealing with the scoundrel just to give Elizabeth some form of peace.

While he was not in a position to give constant friendship, his respect and esteem for her had remained the same even after the excitement of being in her presence, of being the recipient of her dazzling smiles, disappeared. It was love and not mere infatuation, Darcy was quite sure and his heart was utterly broken at the thought of living life without her.

Georgiana saw her brother's ill frame of mind. She attempted to persuade him to return to Hertfordshire and court Elizabeth but he refused to even speak with her about the matter. Darcy tried to hide it, but Georgiana easily saw that he felt guilty for Wickham's actions and believed he was unworthy of Elizabeth's esteem.

Georgiana believed he had entirely mistaken Elizabeth's character. She was too kind to blame Darcy for the situation and sensible enough to see that he was not responsible for the actions of Wickham or any others.

After weeks of arguing with him, Georgiana took matters into her own hands with a timely letter to her cousin Anne. Not only was she certain Darcy and Elizabeth were a perfect match and in a fair way of being in love with one another, she was still determined to have Elizabeth as a sister.

Chapter 7

Elizabeth had felt Darcy's disapproving stare on her when he came to the dinner party before Lydia's wedding. True, several weeks ago she had convinced herself that he admired her, was even humble enough to be interested in her when she had no lofty connections or dowry. Now she knew he was too honourable to stoop so low. Every just feeling must repel the thought of becoming related to Wickham, of attaching himself to a family now touched with scandal.

Although Lydia did not actually engage in anything awful with Wickham, Elizabeth was not at all convinced her sister never would have if given the chance at a later date. What man of sense would bring such a stain to his family in exchange for her sharp words and wilful misunderstandings? She felt as though she could never speak to Darcy again.

It was now six weeks since Lydia had married Wickham and Elizabeth had taken to solitary walks to Oakham Mount, even in the cold early December weather, so she could have the necessary peace required to imagine a life as Mrs. Darcy. It was not fine carriages and jewels of which she dreamed.

For many weeks now she had comprehended that Darcy was exactly the man who, in disposition and talents, would most suit her. His understanding and temper, though unlike her own, would have answered all her wishes. It was a union that must have been to the advantage of both. But no such happy marriage could now teach the admiring multitude what connubial felicity really was due to the preceding marriage of Wickham and Lydia.

Elizabeth was left only with bittersweet memories of a shortened acquaintance. Jane was recently engaged to Bingley and while Elizabeth rejoiced for her sister, she painfully realized that due to Bingley's connection with Darcy she might be thrown into his path again. Pain seared her heart when she thought of witnessing him marry and have children. Unconsciously, tears began to fall on her face.

She could not explain it at all. She had always been sensible and yet somehow she found herself in love with a gentleman she only knew for a matter of days. What started as a vague inclination and admiration for his intellect grew into a stout love.

Recalling her words to Georgiana, which now seemed so long ago, she confessed her love for Darcy was not based at all on the excitement of his attention. She had not seen him in over a month, or heard a thing about him. She was certain she could not be further from his thoughts. With Darcy she had felt at leave to be her true self, a greater friendship she had never known. She felt cherished.

Elizabeth had tried to stop her regard from growing. She knew he could never return it and even if he did matrimony would not follow. There were too many barriers between them and on such a short acquaintance. He owed his family name much more than she could ever bring, especially now. She loved him too much to ask that sacrifice of him. Sometimes it seemed the more she attempted to end her foolish fancy the more it grew.

After a good cry alone on the peak, she resolved to think of it no more. Darcy was not to belong to her and there was nothing to be done for it. Melancholy and sadness would not change a thing. She was not some silly and ignorant girl to be so crossed in love to allow an acquaintance of mere days to affect her entire life.

Upon her return to Longbourn she noticed a grand carriage in the lane. A tall and foreboding woman elegantly dressed, and who might have once been handsome, strutted angrily towards her.

"You must be Elizabeth Bennet. They told me I could find out you outside as you scampered about the countryside like a wild hoyden!"

Elizabeth was not in a mood at all to be so insulted by a stranger. "You have me at a disadvantage for you know my name but I have yet to learn yours."

"Such impertinence! I am Lady Catherine de Bourgh, of course! You must know I am not to be trifled with. A most alarming report reached me two days ago. I was told that your sister is to be most advantageously married and that you would soon be united with my own nephew, Mr. Darcy. I know it must be a falsehood and I insist at once upon having it universally contradicted. Has he, has my nephew, made you an offer of marriage?"

"Did you not just declare it to be impossible? I wonder at you coming at all then." Elizabeth recognized the lady's name as her cousin's patroness. Clearly the Lucases had written the Collinses and some speculation about Elizabeth and Darcy had been made.

How dare they! They base this off of one well chaperoned carriage ride? The man stayed in the area for two days then left for weeks and returned only for my sister's wedding.

"You may have drawn him in with your arts and allurements. I am nearly the closest relation he has and am entitled to know all of his dearest concerns."

"You are certainly not entitled to know mine."

"I am not accustomed to being treated in this manner but I will tell you plainly. This match you desire cannot take place. Mr Darcy is engaged to my daughter."

Elizabeth felt a moment of discomfort at this information but recognized it was similar to what she was told by Wickham, who was entirely discredited. Her belief in Darcy's honour, even if she had no reason to hope he would truly offer to marry her, prevailed.

"If he is then you can have no reason to suppose he would make me an offer."

"The engagement is of a peculiar kind and has been arranged by their respective mothers since their infancy. Do you pay no regard to the wishes of his friends? To his tacit engagement with Miss de Bourgh?

"Are you lost to every feeling of propriety and delicacy? Have you not heard me say that from his earliest hours he was destined for his cousin?"

She testily replied. "Yes, and I had heard it before. But what is that to me? If there is no other objection to my marrying your nephew, I shall certainly not be kept from it by knowing that his mother and aunt wished him to marry Miss de Bourgh. You both did as much as you could in planning the marriage. Its completion depended on others. If Mr. Darcy is neither by honour nor inclination confined to his cousin, why is not he to make another choice? And if I am that choice, why may not I accept him?"

"Because honour, decorum, prudence, nay, interest forbid it. Your alliance will be a disgrace; your name will never even be mentioned by any of us."

"These are heavy misfortunes but the wife of Mr. Darcy must have such extraordinary sources of happiness that she could have no cause to repine."

Lady Catherine's eyes bulged in rage. "If you were sensible of your own good, you would not wish to quit the sphere in which you were brought up."

"He is a gentleman; I am a gentleman's daughter, so far we are equals."

The other woman sniffed. "True. You are a gentleman's daughter. But who was your mother? Who are your aunts and uncles? I am not ignorant of their condition."

"If your nephew does not object to them they can be nothing to you."

Elizabeth's companion seemed to have lost all patience and forthrightly demanded information. "Tell me once and for all, are you engaged to him?"

And people call me impertinent! "I am not." The woman heaved a great sigh.

"And will you promise me to never enter into such an engagement?"

"I will make no promise of the kind. You can have nothing further to say, I will consider this interview over, madam."

Elizabeth began walking back towards Longbourn but the lady called out after her. "I am no stranger to the particulars of your youngest sister's marriage. I know it all; that the young man's marrying her was a patched-up business due to compromise, at the expense of your father and uncles. And is such a girl to be my nephew's sister? Is her husband, is the son of his late father's steward, to be his brother? Heaven and earth! Of what are you thinking? Are the shades of Pemberley to be thus polluted?"

Although incensed and insulted Elizabeth breathed a sigh of relief that Lady Catherine only knew the story explained publically about Lydia's marriage, and that she and her informants did not know the truth of Darcy's involvement.

Not stopping for an instant she only called back, "You have insulted me in every possible method. I must beg to return to the house, but I will never bow to your whims."

"This is your final resolve! Very well. I shall now know how to act. Do not imagine, Miss Bennet, that your ambition will ever be gratified. I came to try you. I hoped to find you reasonable; but, depend upon it, I will carry my point."

The woman talked on in such a manner until they reached her carriage. She turned to Elizabeth and declared, "I take no leave of you, Miss Bennet. I send no compliments to your mother. You deserve no such attention. I am most seriously displeased."

Elizabeth turned on her heel and walked quietly into her house, ignoring her family's demands to know of the visitor. She did not regret a word she said to Darcy's aunt, only that she expressed herself so freely and rudely.

I very much doubt he ever wanted me in the first place but above it all I have now insulted his aunt. Oh, I am such a headstrong, foolish thing!

*****

Darcy sat in his London study having just received a letter from Bingley detailing, between blotches, his engagement to Miss Jane Bennet. He begged for Darcy to return to Netherfield with Georgiana and spend the holidays with Bingley and the Bennets. Caroline would remain in Scarborough and the Hursts would spend the holidays at the Hurst family estate. Bingley desired the company of his closest friend for the festive season.

Darcy intended to decline the invitation. He could not bear to see the look of contempt or sadness in Elizabeth's eyes. He was uncertain how to even maintain his friendship with Bingley in light of his marriage to her dearest sister. He allowed himself to become lost in the memories of Elizabeth and the Gardiner children but was jolted from his reverie due to a commotion in the hall.

The door to his study flung open, his butler nervously hovering behind Lady Catherine de Bourgh.

"It is well, Smith." Darcy tried to reassure his servant that he knew his aunt had made his job impossible.

"Of course it is well." Lady Catherine's voice boomed. She settled herself in a chair and the butler quickly exited and closed the door behind him.

"Aunt, how may I be of service?"

"I have come to put an end to the most slanderous gossip. I have just come from Hertfordshire, where Miss Bennet would not satisfy my inquiries. Obstinate, headstrong girl!"

Darcy was greatly confused. "What is this gossip and how may I end it."

"Announce your engagement to Anne immediately and all shall be rectified."

"I shall not. There is no engagement. There never shall be an engagement. I will not ever marry Anne. You must accept this."

"You would cast aside your duty in favour of a match with this upstart without family or fortune, whose very sister is married in a patched up affair to the son of your father's steward?"

"That is enough, madam! The Bennet family is entirely respectable, the victims of malicious gossip. I owe my family no duty but to marry prudently and Miss Bennet would be a most wholesome match."

"You are then resolved to have her?"

"Certainly not, she is betrothed to my best friend, Bingley. I am only resolved to act in that manner, which constitutes my happiness without reference to you or anyone else so wholly unrelated to the matter."

"No, not Bingley's bride! The impertinent one. There were too many for me to recall their names. But you are no better than she. The unreasonable girl would not oblige me in vowing that any engagement between you two as impossible.

I know it must be so, you could never be taken in by cheap arts and allurements."

Darcy could barely breathe. *Elizabeth would not refuse me?*

"Darcy, the gossip is wild with a match between you two. Anne even has a letter from Georgiana hinting at the idea. That is what set me off more than mere gossip from my parson's family. Georgiana needs a proper model for her coming out. You cannot possibly attach yourself to the Bennet family!"

Georgiana sent a letter to Anne? Now, that is inventive! Touché, little sister!

"I am deeply offended for my friends' sake, as well as my own, madam that you have intruded upon my private affairs and have made horribly unjust accusations at my friends. You shall not be permitted in my homes again until you can make a full apology to the Bennet family. "

Darcy called for his butler to escort the ranting Lady Catherine from his townhouse and quickly wrote a reply to Bingley. He and Georgiana were off for

Hertfordshire at first light the following morning.

*****

The late morning air was unusually warm for December as Darcy espied Elizabeth walking on the path towards Oakham Mount. His feet propelled him, his whole being acting on instinct but he let her reach the top before he quickly outstripped her so he could face her directly. At the sound of his footsteps she looked up at him. Tearstains marked her cheeks.

"Elizabeth," he breathed her name as though it were a prayer.

Elizabeth could not believe her eyes or ears and she was angry at her traitorous heart and her mind for imagining him calling her name. Still astonishment and relief washed over her at the sight of him. She truly hoped he was real.

"Please, dearest, do not cry." Then he took out his handkerchief and tenderly wiped all remnants of her tears away. He was gratified to see affection in her eyes and her warm, broad smile greeted him.

Laughingly Elizabeth said, "I am surprised to see you here, Mr. Darcy. I had heard you did not mean to return to Hertfordshire for quite some time." Then she gave him an impish grin and her eyes twinkled with mischief, his heart soared. "Whatever has happened to your obstinacy, sir?"

"As it turns out I was given new information to change my convictions." He smiled slightly at the ease of their banter, "I had an unexpected visit from my aunt."

"Oh, yes, I did as well."

"Her words taught me to hope as I had scarcely allowed myself to hope before. I can never forgive myself for allowing such a villain to harm your family. Elizabeth if you were not merely espousing false opinions for a debate with my aunt, then you must allow me to tell you how ardently I admire and love you.

"If you will have me, if you will give me your hand, I promise to make you happy and aspire everyday to earn your love and respect. Only you can make me the happiest of men. Marry me?"

Although Elizabeth still wondered how he could possibly offer for her due to Lydia's marriage to Wickham, she did not doubt his constancy. She was his choice, somehow, and she knew he would never waiver from it. There was now no need to address it at the moment.

"Do not dare blame yourself for his actions! You are the most honourable man. Yes, William. I will marry you. You already have my respect and love and only you can make me the happiest of women." Elizabeth smiled as Darcy grinned. She tenderly reached forward to touch his dimples, sighing at the contact.

"Elizabeth, I have a confession to make. I heard you speaking with Georgiana about love months ago."

"Oh, William! We will have to add to your list of faults! You should never eavesdrop!"

Darcy smiled at her tease but persisted with his agenda. "I can think of only one thing to add to your list of understanding infatuation from love; ardent love, that is."

"And what is that, sir?"

"Passion." Elizabeth's breath caught for the fraction of a second she had before Darcy showed her what it meant to be violently in love.

Nine months later

September 21, 1812

"I believe this is my set, Mrs. Darcy."

Mr. Darcy took his beloved's hand and proudly led her to the dance floor. It was not the fashion for married couples to dance, but by now everyone knew to expect Mr. Darcy to dance with his wife, and always the last set.

They had been married over six months but still acted as besotted newlyweds, becoming quite the sensation of the Season. The residents of Meryton found it endearing Mr. and Mrs. Darcy insisted on being present for the Michaelmas Assembly, marking nearly one year since they met.

"You are ever so obstinate in retaining the last set on my card, sir." Elizabeth teased.

"I am quite convinced it is my husbandly right." Darcy grinned.

"We shall leave for Derbyshire on the morrow. Are you certain you shall not mind my cousins visiting us for several weeks?"

Despite the rumours, they had journeyed to Longbourn to celebrate Mr. and Mrs. Bennet's twenty fifth wedding anniversary and needed to return to Pemberley before Michaelmas. The Assembly merely fell on the full moon nearest to the feast day which coincided with the Darcys' stay in the area. The Gardiners were to return with them to Pemberley while Mr. and Mrs. Bennet went on a holiday to the Buxton resort in Derbyshire. Mary and Kitty would travel to Pemberley before going on to visit the Bingleys, new residents of Baxter Hall in Cheshire and only thirty miles from Pemberley.

"How can you ask? I am only sorry Lydia is still in mourning and cannot visit as well. You know how much Georgiana misses her company. I am very surprised at how their temperaments have complimented each other but soon Lydia shall be able to finally move forward with her life."

A brief shadow crossed his face at the remembrance of the pain Wickham inflicted on his family, which now included

Elizabeth's, before he met his fate on a Spanish battlefield in May. Lydia was to stay with her aunt and uncle Phillips while her family travelled.

Rallying his spirits he began again. "And I shall hope your father will surprise us with a visit for I greatly enjoy our debates. But you know I find the Gardiner children delightful, Michael particularly."

Elizabeth lowered her voice and said, "I am glad they shall be visiting. The nursery has needed a good cleaning and airing out. And it shall allow us plenty of time to decorate after they leave."

"Elizabeth! Are you certain now?"

"Yes, love, I felt the quickening this morning."

Darcy smiled broadly and then turned serious, "Come, we are leaving now. You need to rest."

"William, I am perfectly capable of finishing the final set of the evening!"

"No, I insist. We will be travelling for several days and then you shall be hosting our families, you cannot overtax yourself."

"You dare to disagree with your husband? You always were impertinent." Darcy teased with affection.

"And you find it delightful." Elizabeth smiled back.

"As soon as you are rested from our journey I will take you on a long walk near the lake." Darcy smiled with a wistful expression on his face.

"You know I enjoy that walk very much, but why does such a thought enter your head at this moment?"

"Because I need to see you covered in mud as soon as possible. I fell in love with you that day in the park while you were twirling Michael in the air and the thought of you doing so with our children has given me the greatest pleasure for many months now."

Elizabeth smiled at the sentimentality of the great man who had the courage to refute society's prejudices and loved her so selflessly. "And if I refuse? After all, it would not be very dignified for the mistress of Pemberley to have her petticoats six inches deep in mud."

"Have you forgotten my greatest virtue, madam? I am doubly obstinate when perfectly convicted on my decision. And the vision of you dancing in delight with our children heedless of mud and dirt is an image I am certain is most delightful. I am resolved."

They both laughed for a moment before Darcy asked, "What was it Michael said to you before we left this evening?"

"I was speaking with Mrs. Gardiner and gave credit to our fortuitous meeting in the park that day to the weather and remembered you had called it St Michael's Little Summer. We then laughed and recalled Michael's words on the topic, and your gentle manner with him. Then our conversation turned towards their visit to Pemberley. We had not noticed that Michael was nearby. He announced his presence when he declared as he was not an angel after all, he did not need to share his name with the weather anymore."

Darcy lightly chuckled, "Are we to suppose there shall be no warm spells this autumn then?"

"Perhaps not!" Darcy and Elizabeth smiled at each other, both ever sensible to the young boy that was the means of uniting them.

The End

Acknowledgments

This story was inspired by a short challenge piece for an online forum in Autumn of 2013. Since then it has been through over two dozen edits and rewrites and I must thank the encouraging members of BeyondAusten.com, A Happy Assembly, and DarcyandLizzy.com for their kind words. A special thank you to Ecar and Kathy for cold reading this story and for their insightful comments; to Sarah for her support and knowledge of self-publication; and to the Chat Chits who encouraged me during my moments of panic on publishing, or even writing in general.

Thank you to Linda, Jim, Candice, Maartje and Rosie, who were not able to help on this story but have helped and influenced me so much as a writer! Thank you to the countless other people of the JAFF community who have inspired and encouraged me.

Last but not least I could never have written, let alone published, without the love and support of my beloved husband and babies!

About the Author

Rose Fairbanks fell in love with Mr. Fitzwilliam Darcy thirteen years ago. Coincidentally, or perhaps not, she also met her real life Mr. Darcy thirteen years ago. They had their series of missteps, just like Elizabeth and Darcy, but are now teaching the admiring multitude what happiness in marriage really looks like and have been blessed with two children, a four year old son and a two year old daughter.

Previously rereading her favorite Austen novels several times a year, Rose discovered Jane Austen Fan Fiction due to pregnancy-induced insomnia. Several months later she began writing. *The Gentleman's Impertinent Daughter* is her first published work.

Rose has a degree in history and hopes to one day finish her PhD in Modern Europe and will focus on the Regency Era in Great Britain. For now, she gets to satiate her love of research, Pride and Prejudice, reading and writing...and the only thing she has to sacrifice is sleep!

She proudly admits to her Darcy obsession, addictions to reading, chocolate and sweet tea, is always in the mood for a good debate and dearly loves to laugh.

You can connect with Rose on Facebook, Twitter, and her blog: http://rosefairbanks.com.

CPSIA information can be obtained at www.ICGtesting.com
Printed in the USA
BVOW06s0140220516

449059BV00021B/475/P